Tomorrow Is Daddy's Birthday

BY Ginger Wadsworth

ILLUSTRATED BY Maxie Chambliss

BOYDS MILLS PRESS

Text copyright © 1994 by Ginger Wadsworth
Illustrations copyright © 1994 by Maxie Chambliss

Published by Caroline House • Boyds Mills Press, Inc.
A Highlights Company • 815 Church Street
Honesdale, Pennsylvania 18431
Printed in Mexico

Publisher Cataloging-in-Publication Data
Wadsworth, Ginger.
    Tomorrow is daddy's birthday / by Ginger Wadsworth ;
illustrated by Maxie Chambliss.—1st ed.
[32]p. : col. ill. ; cm.
Summary : Tomorrow is Daddy's birthday, and little Rachel
has a present for him. It's a surprise to the reader, until
she whispers her secret to her bunny, the frog, and others.
ISBN 1-56397-042-2
1. Fathers and daughters—Juvenile fiction.
[1. Fathers and daughters—Fiction. 2. Birthdays—Fiction.]
I. Chambliss, Maxie, ill. II. Title.
    [E]—dc20   1994   CIP
Library of Congress Catalog Card Number 92-71870

First edition, 1994
Book designed by Alice Lee Groton
The text of this book is set in 16-point Bookman Light.
The illustrations are done in watercolors.
Distributed by St. Martin's Press

10 9 8 7 6 5 4 3 2 1

After lunch, Rachel wrapped Daddy's present. She stuck on lots of bows and stickers. A roly-poly bug crawled across the floor. Rachel picked up the bug and whispered, "Tomorrow is Daddy's birthday. I'm giving him a . . . and you're the only one who knows. S-sh-h! Don't tell."

Rachel carried the roly-poly bug outside. A frog croaked in the vegetable garden. Rachel squatted between rows of spinach and whispered to the frog, "Tomorrow is Daddy's birthday. You're the only one who knows—except the roly-poly bug. I am giving Daddy something this big." She held up her hands. "S-sh-h! Don't tell."

Rachel unlatched the door of her rabbit's cage. She lifted up one of Fluffy's long floppy ears. "Tomorrow is Daddy's birthday. I am giving him a . . . , " she whispered, "because his old one is broken. You're the only one who knows—except the frog and the roly-poly bug. S-sh-h! Don't tell."

Rachel showed Baby Doll where she had hidden Daddy's present under her bed. "Tomorrow is Daddy's birthday. I'm giving him something he can use every day," she whispered. "You're the only one who knows—except my rabbit Fluffy, the frog, and the roly-poly bug. S-sh-h! Don't tell."

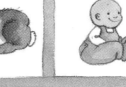

In his bedroom, Rachel's baby brother stacked building blocks on the floor. Rachel sat next to him and whispered, "Andrew, tomorrow is Daddy's birthday. I am giving him a . . . with letters on the side. You're the only one who knows—except Baby Doll, my rabbit Fluffy, the frog, and the roly-poly bug. S-sh-h! Don't tell."

The mailman came to the front door to deliver a package. Rachel told him, "Tomorrow is Daddy's birthday." The mailman leaned down and Rachel whispered in his ear, "I am giving him a . . . and it's blue and white. You're the only one who knows . . . except my brother Andrew, Baby Doll, my rabbit Fluffy, the frog, and the roly-poly bug. S-sh-h! Don't tell."

After dinner, while Mommy read Andrew a bedtime story, Rachel called Grandma. "Tomorrow is Daddy's birthday. I am giving him a . . . , " she whispered into the phone. "You're the only one who knows—except the mailman, Andrew, Baby Doll, my rabbit Fluffy, the frog, and the roly-poly bug. S-sh-h! Don't tell."

Rachel tucked Baby Doll in her little crib. Then Daddy tucked Rachel into her bed.

"How will I know when it's tomorrow, Daddy?"

"When the rooster crows in the chicken house," Daddy answered. He gave Rachel a good-night kiss.

For a long time Rachel was not sleepy. A pale moth fluttered against her little bedside lamp. She whispered to the moth, "Tomorrow is Daddy's birthday. I'm giving him a . . . with a handle. You're the only one who knows—except Grandma, the mailman, Andrew, Baby Doll, my rabbit Fluffy, the frog, and the roly-poly bug. S-sh-h! Don't tell." Rachel snuggled under her quilt.

A rooster crowed in the chicken house near Rachel's window. Rachel opened her eyes. "Today is Daddy's birthday," she told the rooster. "I'm giving him a . . . and I can wash it for him when he is finished. You're the only one who knows—except the moth, Grandma, the mailman, Andrew, Baby Doll, my rabbit Fluffy, the frog, and the roly-poly bug. S-sh-h! Don't tell."

Carrying her present, Rachel hurried into Mommy and Daddy's bedroom. She shook and shook Daddy. "Wake up, wake up, Daddy."

Daddy's eyes opened.

"*Now*, you can open your present," Rachel said.

Daddy sat up and stared at the clock. "It's too early," he moaned.

"Today is your birthday," Rachel said. "And the rooster crowed."

Daddy looked at Mommy, who was still asleep. He looked at the stickers, the bows, and the birthday paper. "I think I need a cup of coffee first."

Rachel giggled.

Daddy and Rachel tiptoed to the kitchen. "I wonder what is in this box?" Daddy said. He pulled off one bow, and then another . . . very slowly.

"Hurry, Daddy, hurry! You can rip the paper."

Finally Daddy opened his present. Inside the paper and ribbons was a beautiful blue-and-white coffee cup with DADDY printed on the side.

"Just what I need! A new cup," Daddy said.

Daddy poured coffee into his new cup. Rachel got out her special dinosaur cup and filled it with orange juice. "Let's clink cups, Daddy, to celebrate."

And they did.